Contents

I0799340

Birds have many body parts.

Animals from Head to Tail

BIRDS FROM HEAD TO TAIL

By Reese Archer

Gareth Stevens
PUBLISHING

Please visit our website, www.garethstevens.com. For a free color catalog of all our high-quality books, call toll free 1-800-542-2595 or fax 1-877-542-2596.

Cataloging-in-Publication Data

Names: Archer, Reese.
Title: Birds from head to tail / Reese Archer.
Description: New York : Gareth Stevens Publishing, 2017. | Series: Animals from head to tail | Includes index.
Identifiers: ISBN 9781482445411 (pbk.) | ISBN 9781482445350 (library bound) | ISBN 9781482445237 (6 pack)
Subjects: LCSH: Birds–Juvenile literature.
Classification: LCC QL676.2 A4753 2017 | DDC 598–dc23

First Edition

Published in 2017 by
Gareth Stevens Publishing
111 East 14th Street, Suite 349
New York, NY 10003

Editor: Ryan Nagelhout
Designer: Katelyn E. Reynolds

Photo credits: Cover, p. 1 Panu Ruangjan/Shutterstock.com; pp. 5, 7, 24 (toucan) PHOTOSVIT/Shutterstock.com; pp. 5, 9 (flying bird) Victor Tyakht/Shutterstock.com; pp. 5, 11, 24 (macaw) TTshutter/Shutterstock.com; pp. 5, 19 (duck) FotoRequest/Shutterstock.com; pp. 5, 21 (peacock) GUDKOV ANDREY/Shutterstock.com; p. 13 John Herd/EyeEm/Getty Images; p. 15 Nagel Photography/Shutterstock.com; p. 17 MollyNZ/iStock/Thinkstock.com; pp. 23, 24 (bald eagle) Phil_Lowe/iStock/Thinkstock.com.

Printed in the United States of America

CPSIA compliance information: Batch #CS16GS: For further information contact Gareth Stevens, New York, New York at 1-800-542-2595.

Birds have hard mouths.
This is called a bill or beak.

Birds have wings.
Most use them to fly!

All birds have feathers.

Robin feathers
are very bright.
They have red chests.

Most birds have four toes.

Some chickens have five!

Ducks have big feet.
They use them to swim.

Peacock tails are huge!
They look like a fan.

Eagles have flat tails.
They use them to fly.

Words to Know

bill

feathers

tail

Index